TOMMY'S MOMMY'S FISH

Nancy Dingman Watson

Illustrated by Thomas Aldren Dingman Watson

VIKING

The illustrations are oil paintings on gessoed illustration board.

VIKING
Published by the Penguin Group
Penguin Books USA Inc., 375 Hudson Street, New York, New York 10014, U.S.A.
Penguin Books Ltd, 27 Wrights Lane, London W8 5TZ, England
Penguin Books Australia Ltd, Ringwood, Victoria, Australia
Penguin Books Canada Ltd, 10 Alcorn Avenue, Toronto, Ontario, Canada M4V 3B2
Penguin Books (N.Z.) Ltd, 182–190 Wairau Road, Auckland 10, New Zealand

Penguin Books Ltd, Registered Offices: Harmondsworth, Middlesex, England

First published in 1971 by The Viking Press
Published with new illustrations in 1996 by Viking,
a division of Penguin Books USA Inc.

1 3 5 7 9 10 8 6 4 2

LIBRARY OF CONGRESS CATALOGING-IN-PUBLICATION DATA
Watson, Nancy Dingman.
Tommy's Mommy's fish / Nancy Dingman Watson;
illustrated by Thomas Aldren Dingman Watson.   p. cm.
Summary: Even though his older brother and sisters
offer to let him share their birthday presents to their mother,
Tommy wants to give her a special present just from him.
ISBN 0-670-85681-9
[1. Birthdays—Fiction. 2. Gifts—Fiction. 3. Fishing—Fiction.]
I. Watson, Thomas Aldren Dingman, ill. II. Title.
PZ7.W328Tq 1996 [E]—dc20 95-50727 CIP AC

Manufactured in China
Set in Planet

Dedicated to Tommy
who really did
make it all happen

My name is Thomas, and once it was my mother's birthday.
I had no present for her, and nobody would take me to the store.
We live on the ocean beach and Tiny's store is in North Truro, and
I could have at least bought her some fishnet, but it's too far to walk.

I asked Cammie, What can I give Mommy for her birthday? She said, Come on, you can help me pick bayberries for a bayberry candle, and we can give it to her together. So I helped Cammie pick bayberries, but I wanted it to be a present all from me, so after a while I quit.

Caitlin was in Brush Hollow picking beach plums, and I said, Cait, what can I give Mommy for her birthday? She said, I'm picking beach plums, and I'm going to make some beach-plum jelly. You can help me, and we can give it to her together. So I helped pick awhile, but I still wanted it to be a present all from me, so I quit.

Peter was sawing wood, and he was going to make his present be a pile of locust logs cut to fit the fireplace. I knew Mommy would like that, and Peter said it could be partly from me if I helped him stack the wood. So I did, but I still wanted it to be a present all from me, so I quit.

I asked Peter what to do.

Peter said, Well, you could draw a picture. So I got out my crayons and I drew a fisherman. But I draw pictures for Mommy every day, and I wanted it to be a special present. So I threw the fisherman away.

Peter said, Why don't you write her a special poem? So I wrote a poem that said I LOVE YOU and some other stuff, but I do that every day anyway, and I didn't want that to be the present. Besides, Caitlin wrote Mommy one that said PLEASE BE MINE OH MOTHER DEVINE and that was much better.

I was getting madder and madder because I couldn't think of a special present for Mommy. Everyone else's present was going to be better than mine and anyway, mine was nothing. That's an awful present.

Then I thought of something neat. I told Peter, I am going to catch Mommy a fish for her birthday. And it isn't going to be any little old sand dabber or a funny-looking thing like a goosefish or a sea robin. It's going to be a STRIPED BASS.

And I told him, Let's go over to the bay side and catch sand eels for bait. Because right now it's low tide, and that's the right time to catch sand eels. Peter said okay, and I let him go along because he let me stack the wood.

We waded up the river, splashing eels out onto the sandbars and catching them when we were quick enough. You can use an eel rake, but it's more fun to grab with your bare hands, and it gives the eels a chance to get away.

The river was full of eels. They jumped all around and the whole world was filled with silvery eels jumping and scooting under the sand and leaping out of the water. They banged into my ankles, and my dog Teddy trapped one under his big front paw for me to use as bait.

Then I had enough eels, so we went back across to the ocean, and when the tide came in high enough, I began to fish. I let Peter cast out for me because he let me help him with the wood, and besides, he likes to see how far out over the surf he can fling the bait.

I fished and fished and after a while Peter had to go finish his chores. But I stayed on fishing because I still didn't have a present all my own for Mommy. The seagulls flew over my head and I counted them.

One for sorrow
Two for joy
Three for a girl
Four for a boy
Five for silver
Six for gold
Seven for a fish you never can hold

I waited till I counted seven birds gliding over me on the wind and then I said it, and I knew I would be catching a big fish before long.

The sun began to go down and the dunes got all pink. The sand-pipers twinkled along the edge of the sea, picking at sand shrimp and teasing Teddy, and he got so mad because he couldn't catch them. He would crouch down and slink along like a tiger till he got close, and then he would burst up in the air and scatter sand all over the place. And the sandpipers just swooped out over the breakers and landed in another spot.

After a while Teddy sat down and stared out over the ocean for a long time, and I knew he felt like giving up.

Once I had a bite and I began to haul it in, but I could tell from the way it dragged it was no striped bass. It was a skate and he was big and heavy, and I finally got him off the hook and I threw him back.

Then I tried casting out all by myself and it was really hard. The first time I caught the hook in the seat of my pants. But I kept trying and I did it right. My line went soaring out over the breakers and just disappeared in the dark water.

Then I waited and waited, and watched the clouds rolling along in the sky and the light shifting on the beach, and pretty soon the sun went down behind the dunes all the way.

Peter came to tell me supper was ready and I should come, and I could give Mommy the wood with him. But I wouldn't quit.

Then Cammie came, and she said I should come, they were all ready to sit down and I could give Mommy the bayberry candle with her. But I wouldn't quit fishing.

Then Cait came, and she said I could give Mommy the beach-plum jelly all from my own self if I wanted, just come because it was almost time for the birthday candles to be lit. But I didn't care. I had to have a present all from me, and it had to be special because it was for Mommy. But I was getting hungry. Besides, said Cait, you're missing the whole party.

Then Cait went away, and the moon began to rise out of the sea, and it made a bright golden path over the water but it was sort of scary too. And then all of a sudden there was a big RACKETY-SPLASHETY way out in the water. Something was jumping and jerking and pulling and splashing at the end of my line, and I began to reel it in. I reeled and I reeled, and I was so afraid it was going to be another skate. But when I got it near shore I could see when the breakers curled up it was a big fat silvery bass. He was giving me a good fight and I was sorry he had to lose, but I was going to win no matter what.

And then guess what happened. That great big bass jumped out of the water and sort of hung there for a second, all silvery in the moonlight. And then he gave a big shiver, and he spit the hook and the bait and everything right out of his mouth and he crashed back into the sea. He was just gone. And you know what? I was glad.

I climbed up the dune and over Brush Hollow and home, and I could see through the window I was just in time for the birthday cake and candles. I went inside and told them what had happened, and everyone cheered for me and my fish. Mommy hugged me and she said it was the best present she ever didn't get in her whole life.

Boy, was I hungry. I had the cake and ice cream first and after that the clam chowder and biscuits. Cait said I smelled all sea-weedy and sand-eely so I sat over by Mommy, and she didn't care how fishy I smelled.